BERNET &ABULI

DARK TALES

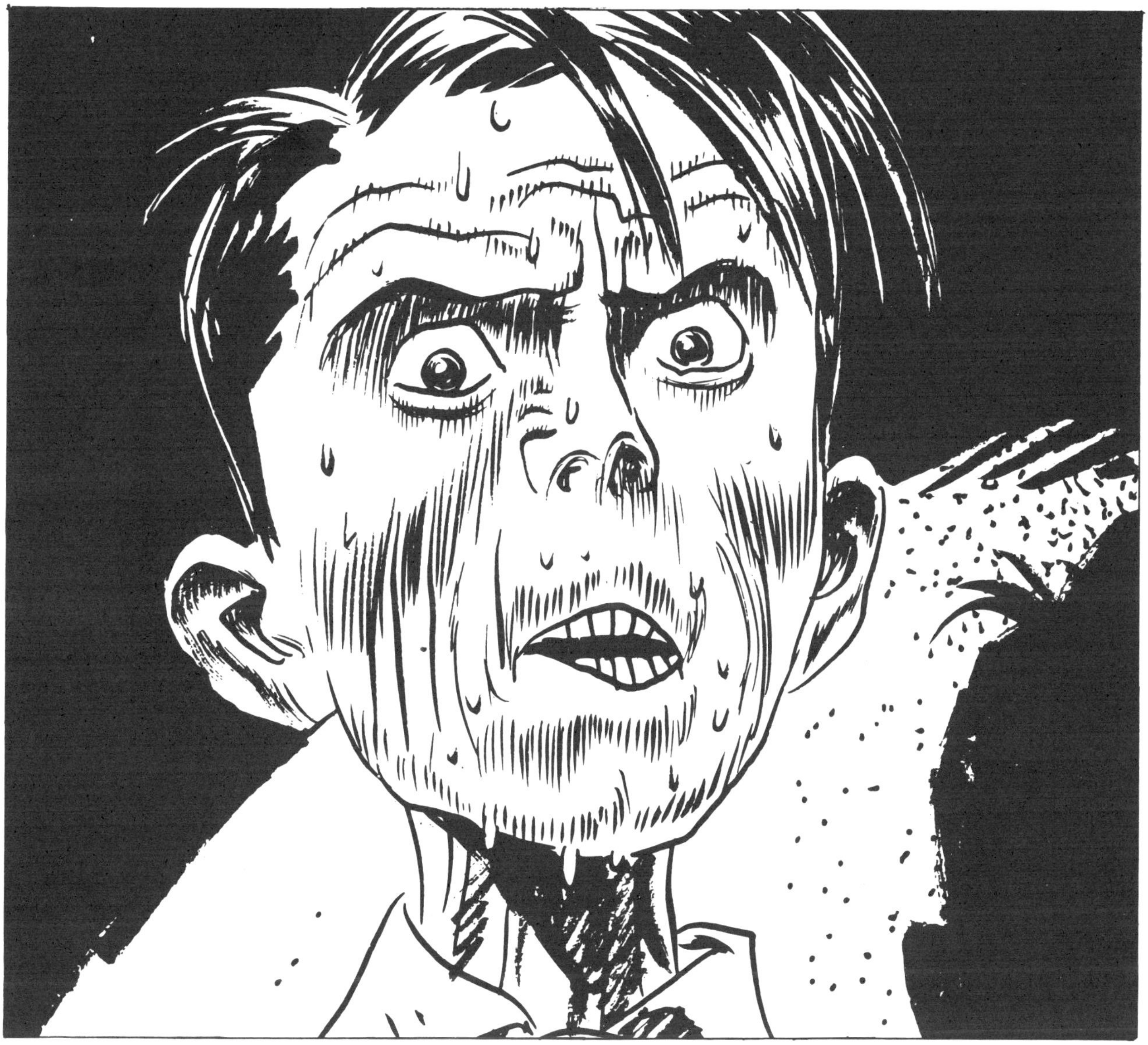

catalan communications
new york

Also Available
by
Bernet & Abuli

TORPEDO 1936 series

by
Jordi Bernet
with
Carlos Trillo

LIGHT & BOLD

DARK TALES
ISBN 0-87416-082-0

Written by E. Sánchez Abuli
Illustrated by Jordi Bernet

Translated by Philip Haworth
Edited by Bernd Metz

Published by Catalan Communications
43 East 19th Street
New York, NY 10003

©1991 Editions Glenat / Comics USA
English Language Edition
©1991 Catalan Communications

First Catalan Communications Edition
March 1991

10 9 8 7 6 5 4 3 2 1

Dep. L.B. 7.148/91
Printed in Catalonia (Spain)

Write to us for a free catalogue, of
our graphic novels,

IT WASN'T MADE FOR ME. IT DOESN'T SUIT ME. IT'S NOT RIGHT. IT'S TOO BIG FOR ME. NO, NOT MY SIZE... THE WORLD.

I'M REALLY NOT MUCH TO LOOK AT. COME CLOSER, GO ON, CLOSER. THERE'S NOT MUCH OF ME.

I'M SMALL...

...LIKE A KID...

BUT I'M NOT A KID. THAT'S THE PROBLEM.

WHERE DO I START? I HAVE TO UNRAVEL THE THREAD OF MY MEMORIES. A BLOOD-RED THREAD WHICH PASSES THROUGH SPOKANE, A CITY ON THE WEST COAST, ASLEEP ON THE BANKS OF A RIVER OF THE SAME NAME.

SPOKANE, ADA, THE BUS. PULLING THE THREAD, I RELIVE THE DRAMA.

EVERY WEDNESDAY, AT THE SAME TIME, SHE ARRIVED ON THE BUS. AND I, ALWAYS PUNCTUAL, WAS WAITING FOR HER.

EVERY WEDNESDAY, IT WAS THE SAME TORTURE, THE SAME OBSESSION. I WAS CRAZY ABOUT HER...

I KNEW HER EVERY STEP, EVERY ROUTINE. THE BUS STOP BY THE SUPERMARKET. THE WEEKLY SHOPPING — FOR ME AN HOUR'S WAIT...

THEN THE BUS AGAIN...

...TO HER HOUSE IN THE COUNTRY WHERE SHE LIVED ALONE...

WEDNESDAY AFTER WEDNESDAY, I FOLLOWED HER. I PROWLED AROUND HER HOUSE LIKE A HUNGRY WOLF. HUNGRY BUT INDECISIVE. WOMEN HAD SCARED ME ALL MY LIFE. I WAS BOTH ATTRACTED TO AND REPULSED BY THEM. BOTH AT THE SAME TIME. NEVER ONE WITHOUT THE OTHER.

AGAIN AND AGAIN I TOLD MYSELF — NEXT WEDNESDAY WITHOUT FAIL. AND WHEN THE DAY CAME...NOTHING. JUST THE SAME STERILE SUFFERING. BUT THIS OBSESSION COULDN'T GO ON FOREVER, IT WAS IMPOSSIBLE.

AND SO THE FATAL WEDNESDAY ARRIVED, FULL OF FEAR AND DESIRE. WAS IT THE WARMTH OF THE EVENING THAT ENABLED ME TO COME A LITTLE CLOSER TO THE HOUSE? I REMEMBER MY SURPRISE WHEN I SAW THE DOOR AJAR...

BUT MY BRAVERY WOULD NEVER HAVE GONE ANY FURTHER IF I HADN'T HEARD...

COME IN!

COME IN!

NO, NO IT WASN'T A DREAM. IT WASN'T MY TORTURED MIND PLAYING TRICKS ON ME. IT WAS HER VOICE, ASKING ME IN...

③

... BUT ENTERING, I DIDN'T SEE ANYONE ...

IN THIS LIFE, THE MOST DIFFICULT THING IS THE FIRST STEP. AFTER THE FIRST COMES THE SECOND. AFTER ONE DOOR, ANOTHER ...

SHE WAS IN THE SHOWER. THAT COULDN'T BE RIGHT. HER VOICE WAS STILL ECHOING IN MY EARS. COME IN. COME IN. NO IT WASN'T A DREAM. SHE'D SAID IT TWICE.

THEN SHE TURNED AROUND, SENSING MY PRESENCE ...

AHHHHHHHHHH!

4

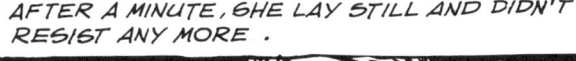

LYING THERE, SHE WAS SO BEAUTIFUL . . .

...SO BEAUTIFUL...

SHE WAS AT MY MERCY AND I TOOK HER. I DID IT TO PUT AN END TO MY OBSESSION, TO EXTINGUISH THE FLAME WHICH WAS DEVOURING ME. AND IN THESE MOMENTS OF HAPPINESS, OF INTENSE JOY, AND OF MADNESS, INTENSE MADNESS, I FELT MYSELF GROWING, GROWING, GROWING . . .

THEN I NOTICED THE FRAGILITY OF HER BODY, JUST AS BEFORE I'D NOTICED THE FRAGILITY OF HER VOICE. WHY TAKE OUT HER HAIR WHICH STILL LAY IN HER THROAT? SHE WAS DEAD.

REPENTANCE CAME LATER, LONG AFTER THE PERVERSITY, LIKE NIGHT FOLLOWS DAY. I HAD TO LEAVE AS QUICKLY AS POSSIBLE.

COME IN.

VENGEANCE

WE'LL IGNORE HOW LOBOS HAD EVADED THE VIGILANCE OF THE GUARDS AND ENTERED THROUGH THE WINDOW OF THE CAPTAIN'S HOUSE. HE FOUND THE OFFICER FAST ASLEEP. WITHOUT HESITATION, HE TOOK OUT HIS KNIFE AND PLUNGED IT INTO THE CHEST OF THE SLEEPING MAN.

ABULÍ / BER NET

AS HE WAS LEAVING, HE MADE SOME NOISE AND WAS ARRESTED.

LATER, DURING A SUMMARY TRIAL HE WAS SUBJECTED TO . . .

YOU KILLED CAPTAIN VINETA, YES OR NO?

YES, I KILLED HIM AND I'D DO IT AGAIN IF I COULD.

THE SENTENCE WAS NEVER IN DOUBT. A SQUAD UNDER THE COMMAND OF LIEUTENANT RODRIGUEZ, LED THE PRISONER INTO THE WOODS TO BE SHOT.

YOUR LAST REQUEST, REBEL!

AS LOBOS MADE HIS DEMAND, NO MORE, NO LESS, THE TRAGEDY WAS BORN...

HA! HA! HA! HA! HA! HA!

HA! HA! HA!

SHUT UP!

DON'T LET HIM OUT OF YOUR SIGHT, I WON'T BE LONG.

THE OTHER MEN WHO HAD BEEN SHOT USUALLY RESTRICTED THEMSELVES TO A LAST CIGARETTE OR A FEW SECONDS IN PRAYER.

BUT THE DAMN REBEL HAD MADE HIS DEMAND. IF HE THOUGHT THAT RODRÍGUEZ WOULD CHICKEN OUT, HE WAS WRONG. NO PROVOCATION COULD MAKE HIM FLINCH.

GRAN CORRIDA

DOMINGO TOROS

PULQUES FINOS

2

MONEY COULDN'T DO ANYTHING. SHE EVEN SAID THAT IT WOULD BE LIKE SLEEPING WITH A PRIEST. IT WOULD BRING HER BAD LUCK TO GO AGAINST THE WILL OF GOD. SHE HAD NO DESIRE TO INCUR GOD'S WRATH.

NO PUSSY FOR THE REBELS!

GOD DIDN'T MAKE THESE BEAUTIES FOR THOSE BASTARDS!

IN THE VILLAGE SQUARE, RODRIGUEZ STARTED A RUMOR THAT THERE WAS A REWARD FOR THE WOMAN WHO WOULD DO THE DEED.

CANTINA

3

HERE'S THE THE LIEUTENANT!

THE MEN'RE GETTING RESTLESS LIEUTENANT. SHALL WE SHOOT HIM?

NO ONE'S SHOOTING ANYONE TILL WE GET A WOMAN.

THE LIEUTENANT'S RAGE AMUSED LOBOS. DYING DIDN'T BOTHER HIM MUCH. WHAT DID HE HAVE ON EARTH? NO PARENTS, NO FRIENDS, NO WOMAN. NOT EVEN A DOG WHICH WOULD WAG ITS TAIL WHEN IT SAW HIM. A BALL AND CHAIN, THAT'S WHAT HIS LIFE HAD BEEN.

HE HAD ALREADY ACCOMPLISHED HIS LAST WISH IN ASSASSINATING THE GOOD CAPTAIN. HE HAD ONLY MADE THE REQUEST TO ANGER THE LIEUTENANT, NOT TO PROLONG HIS LIFE AIMLESSLY. WHY WERE THEY WAITING TO KILL HIM?

SHE ARRIVED LIKE THE FIRST LIGHT OF DAWN. SHE WAS SO BEAUTIFUL THAT, LATER, THE SOLDIERS THOUGHT THEY'D BEEN DREAMING.

I'VE COME FOR THE REWARD.

TELL YOUR MEN TO DRAW BACK, LIEUTENANT, THIS ISN'T A CIRCUS ACT.

IT'S DEATH.

5

NO, SHE'S TOO BEAUTIFUL. SHE CAN ONLY BE LIFE.

THEN THEIR LIPS MET. TWO BREATHS MERGING, TWO BODIES TOUCHING, TWO FACES WITH THE SAME DESIRE... TO JOIN AS ONE. ONE YOU, ONE ME AND THE ENTIRE WORLD.

IMMEDIATELY, LOBOS HAD THE FEELING THAT THESE LIPS WERE NOT KISSING HIM OUT OF HABIT. HE REALISED, CONFUSEDLY, THAT THE REWARD HAD CONTRIBUTED NOTHING TO THE ARDOR OF THE KISSES SHE WAS GIVING HIM – IT WAS SOMETHING ELSE.

THE REBEL KNEW NOW THAT HIS LIFE HAD BEEN USELESS, THAT THE CARESSES HE HAD KNOWN DID NOT COUNT, THAT HE HAD NEVER BEEN IN ANY OTHER ARMS, THAT NO OTHER WOMAN HAD EXISTED EXCEPT THIS STRANGER.

WHAT COULD HE KNOW ABOUT THIS FLOWER HE HAD PICKED? DO YOU LOVE ME? DO YOU LOVE ME NOT? INSTANTLY, HE WAS SURE THAT SHE LOVED HIM. MY GOD, THIS WOMAN LOVED HIM. AND IT WAS TOO LATE!

6

THAT'S IT! ENOUGH NOW!

DEATH NO LONGER HELD ANY ATTRACTION FOR LOBOS. JUST AS HE THOUGHT HE HAD SATISFIED HIS APPETITE, HE FELT THE BIRTH OF A NEW APPETITE WHICH WAS STRONGER THAN ANYTHING.

YOU LOVE ME!

7

IT AFFECTED HIM SO STRONGLY HE HAD TO BE BOUND.

YOU LOOO-VE MEEE!

ON THE LIEUTENANT'S ORDER, SIX GUNS WERE POINTED AT HIM.

NOOOO!

TAKE AIM!

I BEG YOU...

FIRE!

AND SO LOBOS DIED, A PRIMROSE OF FIVE RED PETALS SPREAD ON HIS CHEST.

THE REWARD.

BUY SOME FLOWERS FOR THE DECEASED.

FROM WHO, MADAM?

FROM THE CAPTAIN'S WIDOW.

BER NET

8

LOVE STORY

SO, WHAT HAPPENED?

CALM DOWN, GUYS, CALM DOWN. LET'S BEGIN AT THE BEGINNING. HELP ME FIND CHARLIE.

HELLOOO!

CHARLIE!

WHERE'RE YOU HIDING, CHARLIE?

CLANK

CHARLIE! CHARLIE!

CHARLIE! CHARLIE!

COMING MR. HANSEN! COMING!

NO! NO! NO!

NOOOO!

HUH?

DR. BERNSTEIN'S ARTIFICIAL LEGS REVOLUTIONIZE MEDICINE.

DON' BOTHA READIN' THA-A-T. FORGEDD IT. IT'LL CO-OST A FORT-OON!

5

27

28

32

MEOW!

SHHH!

I'M SLEEPING. DON'T SPEND THE NIGHT WORKING. DON'T LEAVE THE DISHES. DON'T WAKE ME UP. DON'T SNORE. FEED THE CAT.

MEE-EEE-OWWW!

SHH-SHH!

I THINK YOU'RE PUTTING ON WEIGHT.

THE MARTIANS! THE MARTIANS ARE COMING!

WRRRAAAAAAAAAAAAAAA

PATCHULI

BUT, JOEY, IT AIN'T MINE!

HE WENT WHERE HE HAD TO GO . . .

ME, A MONSTER!

STUP!

BANG BANG

BUT THINGS TURNED SOUR. THE POLICE WERE WAITING . . .

WAAAAH WAA

BANG BANG BANG

THEY DIDN'T MISS... HE ENDED UP LIKE A RAT IN THE GUTTER.

WAAAH WAAAAH

WHY DID THE PUMP GUY SAY JOEY WAS A MONSTER? HE WAS CUTE! HE WAS A TOUGH GUY, THAT'S ALL. THE PUMP GUY WAS A TOUGH GUY, TOO... 'CEPT HE TOLD THE COPS.

BUMMER! THREE SHOTS IN HIS ASS FOR CALLING JOEY A MONSTER. IT SUCKS. BUT IT SUCKS FOR JOEY AS WELL, GETTING KILLED'N'ALL.

HI, GUYS!

WAIT FOR ME!

WAIT FOR ME, DEE DEE, WAIT FOR ME!

BER NET

8

46

47